This book belongs to:

D1398227

SCOOBY-DOO!™

Vanishing Apples

By Gail Herman
Illustrated by Duendes del Sur

Advance PUBLISHERS

Scooby-Doo!

READ & SOLVE

Find These Fun Activities Inside!

Check the inside back cover for fun things to do!

Bonus story-related activity strips throughout the 15 volumes.

Create your own mystery book, *Scooby-Doo The Swamp Witch!* Color, collect, and staple the coloring pages at the end of the first 12 books in the Scooby-Doo Read & Solve mystery series.

Copyright © 2006 Hanna-Barbera.
SCOOBY-DOO and all related characters and elements are trademarks of and © Hanna-Barbera.
WB SHIELD: ™ & © Warner Bros. Entertainment Inc.
(s08)

ADVANCE PUBLISHERS

www.advancepublishers.com
Produced by Judy O Productions, Inc.
Designed by SunDried Penguin Design
All rights reserved.
Printed in China

Scooby-Doo and Shaggy jumped
out of the Mystery Machine.
"Like, any pizza around here?"
asked Shaggy. "I'm starving."
"Rizza! Rizza!" Scooby said.

COUNTING MYSTERY

How many buckets
are in this book?

The rest of the gang
climbed out of the van.
Velma laughed. "There's no pizza here."
"This is an apple orchard," Fred added.
"That's right," said Daphne. "We're here
to pick apples."

Answer: 12

"We're here to *pick* apples?" Shaggy moaned. "Not eat them?"
"That comes later," Daphne promised.

5

"Like, I'm so hungry," Shaggy said. "I'm going to pick more apples than anyone!"

"Don't be so sure." Velma smiled. "I've read books about picking apples. I know exactly how to do it."

Shaggy looked at her. He was much taller than Velma was. He could reach more apples.

"Let's have a contest," he said. "We can split into groups. And the winners get to eat all the apples!"

"I don't know," said Velma. "This is a big place. Maybe we should stay together. So we don't get lost."

Shaggy pictured apple pies and apple jam. Scooby pictured candy apples and sweet applesauce. "Ro way!" said Scooby.

8

"Then let the contest begin!" said Velma.
Everyone took baskets. Shaggy and Scooby went one way. Daphne led Fred and Velma the other way.

Shaggy reached for apples way
up high. Scooby bent for apples way down low.
One by one, they put them in the basket.

10

A little later, Shaggy checked the basket.
"Zoinks!" he cried. "It's empty!"

Shaggy eyed Scooby. "Did you eat the apples?"

"Ro ray," said Scooby. "Rou ate the rapples!"

"Like, no way for me, too!" Shaggy said.

They both shrugged. "Let's start over," said Shaggy.

They reached and pulled and picked and tossed.

Shaggy peeked in the basket.

Empty again!

"Scooby, stop eating the apples!" Shaggy cried.

Scooby shook his head. "Rou rop eating!"

"*You're* not eating the apples," said Shaggy.

"And *I'm* not eating the apples. So who's eating the apples?"

SEEK & FIND

Find the jar of apple jam on this page, and then find four more on the following pages.

All at once, Scooby shivered. It was getting cold. The sun was going down.

They needed apples to win the contest. But the apples kept disappearing!

"We have to figure this out," said Shaggy. "Before it is too late."

"Who did this?" Shaggy called out.
"Who?" A voice called back.
Shaggy and Scooby jumped.
Someone was teasing them.
But they couldn't see anybody.

"We should call the police!" said Shaggy.

"*Call!*" said a voice.

They peered into the darkness. Still no one.

17

"Someone is out there," Shaggy said. "But we can't see him. He must be invisible!"

All of a sudden, an apple hit Shaggy on the head.
"Ouch!"
An apple hit Scooby on the head.
"Rouch!"

"It's an apple attack!" Shaggy cried. Apples crashed down, one after the other. "Run for your life, Scoob old buddy," Shaggy said.

They turned to speed away. But they slipped on wet leaves.

Find the difference between Scooby on this page and the one below.

Crash! They bumped into something … big … tall … Giant arms trapped them. "It's the invisible man!" Shaggy shouted. They tumbled to the ground in a heap.

Answer: missing spots on arm, missing Scooby tag, scarf has purple stripes

Boom! Boom! They heard thudding footsteps. Breaking branches.
But they couldn't see a thing. More invisible people!
"It's a whole army!" Shaggy wailed. "We're goners!"

"Jinkies!" said a voice. "We finally found you!"

"The invisible man sounds just like Velma!" said Shaggy.

Velma pulled a wet leaf from Shaggy's eyes. "It *is* Velma," she said.

"What?" Shaggy leaped to his feet. "You're all here! You must have scared away the invisible men."

Shaggy explained about the missing apples. The voices teasing them. The apples hitting them on the head. The giant arms grabbing them.

Velma pushed away two branches.
"These are your giant arms. You ran
into a tree. But you couldn't tell
because leaves covered your eyes."

26

"Who! Call!" the voices said again.

"Hmm," said Velma. "That 'whoooo' sounds like a hoot. And the 'call'? That sounds like *caw*."

"An owl and a crow!" Daphne exclaimed.

Next, Velma picked up the basket. "Aha! There's a hole in it! That's why the apples disappeared. They kept falling out!"

"But what about the apple attack?" Shaggy asked as another apple hit his head. "Ouch!"

Fred grinned. "The apples are ripe."

"That's right," Velma agreed. "The wind blows them down. Or they fall on their own."

The mystery was solved. But now it was so dark, the gang could hardly see.

"How will we find our way back?" asked Daphne.

"Look at this, Scoob!" said Shaggy. "All our apples! In a row!"

"It's like a trail," said Velma. "We can follow the apples to find our way back."

MYSTERY MIX-UP?

Unscramble the letters to solve these word mysteries.

rocdahr

tkaebs

wlo

agtin

lpeap

gkcpini

Answer: orchard, basket, owl, giant, apple, picking

"But," said Shaggy, "how do we know who wo[n]
the contest?"

Velma grinned. "You can walk, eat, and count [at]
the same time."

"One." *Crunch.* "Two." *Crunch.*

"Scooby-Dooby Doo!"

SCOOBY-DOO!

Create your own bonus book!

Step 1:
Color both sides of this storybook page.

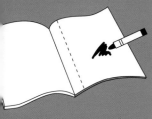

Step 2:
With an adult's supervision, carefully cut along the dotted line.

Step 3:
Repeat steps 1 and 2 on the first 12 books of the Scooby-Doo Read & Solve mystery series.

Please turn page over for further instructions.

"Mrugorowl-ow-ow-owl!" cried the zombie.
"R-run, Scoob!"
"Ruh-huh!"

Meanwhile, the rest of the gang found some mysterious stuff.

"A winch... power tools... and a cutting torch," said Fred.
"What would a witch want with a winch in a swamp?" asked Daphne.
"I wonder..." thought Velma.

Step 4:
Put all 12 cut-out pages neatly in order.

Step 5:
Staple three times on the left side of the paper stack to create the book's spine.

Step 6:
Congratulations, you have solved the mystery!

You have now created your very own Scooby-Doo storybook!